This book is given to:

_____

from:

_____

Dedication:
To Mom and Dad,
for teaching me by example how
to love people of every race.

Published by B&H Publishing Group,
Nashville, Tennessee

All Scripture quotations are taken from the Christian
Standard Bible®, Copyright © 2017 by Holman Bible Publishers.
Used by permission. Christian Standard Bible® and CSB® are
federally registered trademarks of Holman Bible Publishers.

DEWEY: 177   SBHD: RACE/RACE AWARENESS/FRIENDSHIP

Printed in January 2018 in Shenzhen, Guangdong, China

1 2 3 4 5 6 • 22 21 20 19 18

ColorFull

Celebrating the Colors God Gave Us

Dorena Williamson

Illustrated by Cornelius Van Wright and Ying-Hwa Hu

B&H
PUBLISHING GROUP
Nashville, Tennessee

Summer had finally arrived! Imani was excited to blow bubbles and jump on the trampoline and climb trees. She and her little brother, Christopher, were waiting for their friend Kayla to join in the fun.

"Hi guys! Wanna see who can blow the biggest, most poppable bubble?" asked Kayla as she climbed over the fence.

"Wow, look at my bubble!" said Christopher. "It's full of swirly colors!"

"I've got colors floating on mine too!" Kayla added.

"I never knew bubbles
could have so many colors!"
said Imani.

"Well, you all are amazing bubble makers!" said Granny Mac, walking outside to join the kids.

"Look!" said Christopher. "My bubble is ginormous and has fifty gazillion colors in it!"

"How about that!" said Granny Mac. "Aren't colors wonderful?"

"Mine has pink and purple—my favorite!" said Kayla.

"Well, isn't that something?" said Granny Mac. "Right in this backyard, what other colorful things do you see?"

"I see Mama's flowers! Lots of orange and yellow!" said Imani.

Kayla ran toward the garden. "And I see red tomatoes and green beans!"

"Does gray count?" asked Christopher. "Because I see a crazy gray squirrel running up that tree!"

"Yep! Gray is a color too. And I think it's a rather pretty one," said Granny Mac, patting her silvery hair.

"Close your eyes," she said. "Imagine if you couldn't see any of the colorful things around you. No blue sky, no white clouds, no crazy gray squirrel.

"Now, open your eyes and enjoy the view! God did wonderful work making His creation so colorful! Wouldn't it be sad to miss out on all this beauty He made?

Imani looked around and thought for a second. "Yep, this is much better than being in the dark!"

"You guys are probably thirsty after all that color hunting. Come have a snack . . . I want to tell you something else that is very special about God's creation.

"We just saw how God painted vivid colors. He did that on purpose, making everything in the earth and sky a special color.

"Now, when God created people, He didn't make us all one color either, did He?" asked Granny Mac.

"No, ma'am. God made my skin chocolate just like yours!" said Christopher with pride.

"That's right," chuckled Granny Mac. "God decided chocolate was the right skin color for you. And Imani, even though you and Christopher are in the same family, your caramel-colored skin is different than his."

"What about me, Granny Mac?" asked Kayla, her eyes wide.

"Dear girl, God decided you would look beautiful with vanilla-colored skin."

"And red hair!" added Kayla.

"Absolutely, hair the color of the rising sun," said Granny Mac with a smile.

"God must love color to have made all of earth's people
with such wonderful shades. That's something to celebrate!

"We can celebrate all our differences—the color of our skin, the texture of our hair, the shape of our eyes, nose, and lips. Every single person is part of God's grand design!"

"Sometimes people say we should be color*blind* and not notice the different colors of our skin. But God gave us eyes to take in all His wonderful colors.

Why would we want to be blind and not see them?"

"So if we aren't colorblind, then what are we?" asked Kayla.

Granny Mac declared, "Well, our eyes are full of all the colors God made, and our hearts are full of celebration for all that color. So that means we are colorFULL!"

"Yeah, baby, we're not colorblind, we're colorFULL," said Christopher.

"You know what else has color?"
asked Granny Mac. "Ice cream!"
"Whoopee!" said the kids.

"Look," said Imani, "all our ice cream
is colorFULL too!"

"Being colorFULL sure does
taste good," said Christopher.

"I agree," said Granny Mac. "Being colorFULL is one of God's sweetest gifts."

Remember:

I will praise you because I have been remarkably and wondrously made. Your works are wondrous, and I know this very well.
—Psalm 139:14

Read:

Read Acts 10:24–28. Peter was one of Jesus' disciples and watched his Master cross cultural barriers. Jesus gave Peter and many others the Great Commission to go and make disciples of all nations (Matthew 28:19-20), and Peter had preached to an ethnically diverse crowd on the day of Pentecost (Acts 2). Yet when we get to Acts 10, he is still dividing the Jews and Gentiles. As God leads Peter to the home of a Gentile named Cornelius, Peter has a defining moment and declares that God has shown him that no race is better than any other (v. 28).

God wants us to understand His intent in creating *everything* good—including every person in the world. We are all remarkably and wondrously made!

Think:

1. Think about all the people you know. How many different skin, hair, and eye colors can you count?

2. In the story, Imani and Kayla are best friends. How are they alike? How are they different?

3. Granny Mac reminds the kids that God chose their unique hair and skin colors. Why do you think God chose the colors He picked especially for you?

4. Imagine a world with no color. What would it be like? Would it be happy or sad? Why?

5. Why do you think God created a world and people with so many wonderful colors? Can you think of a way to celebrate our beautifully different skin colors?

6. Think about the meanings of the words *blind* and *full*. Would you rather be color*blind* or color*full*? Why?